Adventures in Recess
The Boys

Written by Mari Lumpkin
Illustrated by Natalia Buscaglia

FLYING TURTLE
PUBLISHING

Acknowledgement

To Antoinette Horton, my Mom,
who inspired this book.
And to Allen, Bradley and Diego, the Three
Amigos whose friendship gave her the idea.

FLYING TURTLE
PUBLISHING

Adventures in Recess: The Boys copyright © 2015 by Mari Lumpkin.
Revised edition published by Flying Turtle Publishing, May 2017.

This book is a work of fiction. Any references to historical events, real people, or real locales are used fictitiously. Other names, characters, places, and incidents are the product of the author's imagination, and any resemblance to actual events or locales or persons, living or dead, is entirely coincidental.

The publisher does not have any control over third-party websites or their content. All rights reserved, including the right of reproduction in whole or in part in any form, without written permission from the publisher.
If you purchased this book without a cover, you should be aware that this book is stolen property.

It was reported as "unsold and destroyed" to the publisher, and neither the author nor the publisher has received any payment for this "stripped" book. Please do not participate in or encourage piracy of copyrighted materials in violation of authors' rights.

Manufactured in the United States of America

Publisher's Cataloging-in-Publication data
Names: Lumpkin, Mari, author.
Title: Adventures in Recess / by Mari Lumpkin; illustrated by Natalia Buscaglia.
Description: Hammond, IN: Flying Turtle Publishing, 2015. | Summary: Join the fun when three best friends—Allen, Bradley and Diego—
use their imaginations to re-invent recess.
Identifiers: LCCN 2015952546 | ISBN 978-0-9911378-8-6 (hardcover) |
ISBN 978-0-9911378-9-3 (paperback)
BISAC : JUV001000 JUVENILE FICTION | Action & Adventure | General

Adventures in Recess: The Boys is available at special discounts when purchased in bulk for premiums, promotions and for fund-raising or educational use.
Contact Mari Barnes at ftpublish@gmail.com.

Chapter 1
Monday

Bradley watched his older brother, Abram. Abram caught a ball and ran past. "Bradley, don't get your head stuck in that fence again," Abram called.

Allen and Diego went to their friend.

"What's the matter?" Allen asked. Bradley leaned against the fence. He looked so sad.

"We do the same things every day—tag, kickball, swings. I want to do something different."

"We could play kickball but run backwards. That would be different," Allen suggested.

2

"No, I mean something exciting." Bradley stood on the fence rail.

His two friends joined him. Allen said, "Let's go around the schoolyard without getting down. Come on!"

He moved slowly. Reach, grab, pull, step. The others followed.

"Look down. What do you see?" Diego asked.

"Rocks," Bradley answered.

"Dangerous rocks. The biggest I've ever seen!" Diego smiled.

Bradley and Allen looked down again.

"And wild animals!" Diego pointed.

"Those are ants." Bradley frowned.

"No, they are hungry alligators. We must stay on this bridge to be safe!"

Bradley looked even more confused. "What?"

"We've got to use this shaky bridge to cross the river." Allen nodded his head.

"What?"

Allen put one hand on Diego's shoulder and yelled, "Imagination activation!"

Diego put one hand on Bradley's shoulder. "Imagination activation!"

Now, Bradley could see it all. The wild water swirled far below. Alligators splashed and snapped.

The boys held on tight and inched toward the other side.

"We have to capture the giant snake. It's been eating the great eagle's eggs." Allen pointed to a bird flying overhead.

"Hold on," Bradley called. "The wind is blowing harder." He swayed back and forth. Allen and Diego swayed too.

Allen said, "Oh, no! The eagle thinks we're after her eggs." He ducked and the others ducked too. Then they moved on.

"I think I see it. It's incredible!" Diego pointed.

"The King Kokomoko Snake. The biggest snake in the world," Allen said.

Bradley whispered, "We've got to take it by surprise. Ready, set, jump!"

They leaped onto the snake's back. It twisted and rolled to throw them off. The boys hung on.

They lifted the snake high above their heads just as the bell rang.

Chapter 2
Tuesday

Allen, Bradley and Diego ran to a corner of the playground.

"Yesterday was the best recess ever!" Allen jumped up and down. "Where are we going today?"

A piece of paper floated over the fence. Bradley caught it and headed for the recycle bin.

"What is that?" Allen asked.

Bradley said, "It's just a sales flyer for the Green Grass Grocery Store."

Diego took the paper and smoothed it against the ground. "No, it's a map. A treasure map!"

They put their arms around each other's shoulders. "Imagination activation!"

"I see it now." Diego held the map in both hands. "This will lead us to the

treasure of Gold Hook the Pirate. See, we start at the Hopscotch Hills."

"We have to be careful," Bradley said. "The people in those hills are not always friendly. We have to hop along the path."

The people of Hopscotch Hill were NOT friendly at all. They frowned and hollered and pushed.

"Hey, go away. We're playing here!"

"Move! It's my turn!"

"Mrs. Merkle, these boys are bothering us!"

The boys moved fast. They checked the map again.

"We have to get past the Swinging Soldiers. They guard the gates to the Magic Mountain. I'll go first." Allen was the smallest, but he was a fast runner.

"Be careful and good luck." Bradley and Diego shook his hand. Allen ran.

The Swinging Soldiers tried to stop him. Allen was just out of their reach.

"Come on, you can do it," Allen called to his friends. "Just stay low."

It was close, but Bradley and Diego made it.

Diego gave them good news. "We're almost there. All we have to do is climb the mountain and slide down. The treasure is in the valley of Green Grass."

The snow was deep on Magic Mountain. It was hard to take every step. Bradley looked back and yelled, "Hurry. A pack of polar bears is coming up behind us!"

The boys whizzed down a winding trail and into the valley.

"There it is!" Diego pointed to a tree.

They found Gold Hook's treasure just in time.

Chapter 3
Wednesday

Diego, Bradley and Allen rushed to the playground. They huddled and shouted, "Imagination activation!"

"We're getting pretty good at this," Allen said. He looked at his friends and smiled.

"Wow, we look awesome!" Bradley twirled around. His cape floated on the breeze. "I am Green Lightning. I strike down the bad guys!"

"I'm the Dragonfly, fearless and fast!" Allen ran to the fence and back.

"I am El Campeón, brave and bold!" Diego struck a superhero pose. "Señor Stinker and his crew are hiding somewhere close."

"They're going down," Bradley said in a growly voice. "But how will we find them?"

"Listen!" Allen cupped a hand around his ear. "I hear a secret message with my super hearing."

A teacher was sharing nursery rhymes. "One-two, buckle my shoe. Three-four, shut the door. Five-six, pick up sticks. Seven-eight, lay them straight."

Allen nodded. "That's the code. It will help us find Señor Stinker."

The boys flew around in search of a shoe to buckle. After a while, they stopped to rest.

Dragonfly asked, "Who wears shoes with buckles? Laces or Velcro, sure. Nobody wears buckles."

"I see one with my super sight!" Green Lightning pointed to a small girl. The strap on her shoe flapped with every step she took.

She smiled and said, "Thank you," when he closed the buckle.

"What's next?" El Campeón asked. "It was 'three-four…'"

A door slammed. A car drove off.

Speeding to the fence, Green Lightning said, "Oh, no, Señor Stinker is getting away!"

"There's our next clue." Dragonfly pointed to some scattered twigs.

"Five-six, pick up sticks. Seven, eight, lay them straight." The heroes finished the rhyme. They looked at the line of sticks at their feet.

"I don't see how this helps us get the bad guys. Dragonfly, use your super hearing," said El Campeón.

"Yesterday, upon the stair, I met a man who wasn't there. He wasn't there again today. I wish that man would go away," the teacher said. Dragonfly repeated each word.

"'A man who wasn't there?' What kind of man is that?" El Campeón stared down at the line of sticks. It pointed to Green Lightning's shadow.

"They're hiding in the shadows. Get them!" The superheroes chased the bad guys into the sunlight.

The bad guys faded away. The boys had saved the world!

Chapter 4
Thursday

Rain poured from the sky in cold gray sheets. Today, recess would be in the gym. How could Allen, Bradley and Diego have an adventure inside?

Mr. Lokken, the gym teacher, said, "We're going to have a relay race. I want four students on each team."

The boys looked at each other. There were only three of them. Kids scrambled to pick their teams.

"I'll help you choose if you need help," Mr. Lokken said. Finally, only Lila and Patti waited.

No one wanted Lila on their team. She was taller than most of class. She was mean and teased everyone.

No one wanted Patti either. She was short and chunky. Her glasses always slid down her nose.

Bradley and Allen stared at their shoes. Diego called, "We take Patti." He didn't want Lila. She made fun of him when he spoke.

"This is a special relay," Mr. Lokken told the class. "The first part has hurdles, up and back. Tag your teammate. The next two students run up and back. Tag your teammate each time. That's important."

The boys whispered, "Imagination activation!"

Patti smiled. "Wow, we look so cool! Green and blue are my favorite colors."

"You can see our uniforms?" Allen asked.

Patti stretched her arms wide. "I can see everything. There are crowds in the stands and flags from different countries. It's the Olympics!"

"How?" Bradley asked.

"Patti has *una gran imaginación,* a big imagination." Diego smiled.

"The last part of the race is the obstacle course. The runner can't miss any of them." Coach Lokken blew his whistle and started his stopwatch. The race was on!

Allen sailed over the first hurdles with ease. Then he tripped and had to try again.

Diego went next. He sprinted to the far wall and zoomed back. Bradley jumped and yelled, "Come on, Diego!" Then he took off so fast that Diego didn't get to tag him.

Coach Lokken blew his whistle. "Bradley, get back here. You have to be tagged."

They were falling behind and the boys were worried. Patti had to run the obstacle course. The hardest part.

"Bradley, tag me!" she called. Patti started racing. Very slowly.

Everyone was screaming for their teammates to go faster. Allen, Bradley and Diego were quiet. They didn't believe that Patti would finish the race before school ended for the day.

Patti stepped into every ring on the floor. She carefully moved between each orange cone. Some of the children ran so fast that they missed a ring or a cone. Some bumped into each other and fell down.

Patti didn't miss a thing.

Bradley yelled, "Look at her go!"

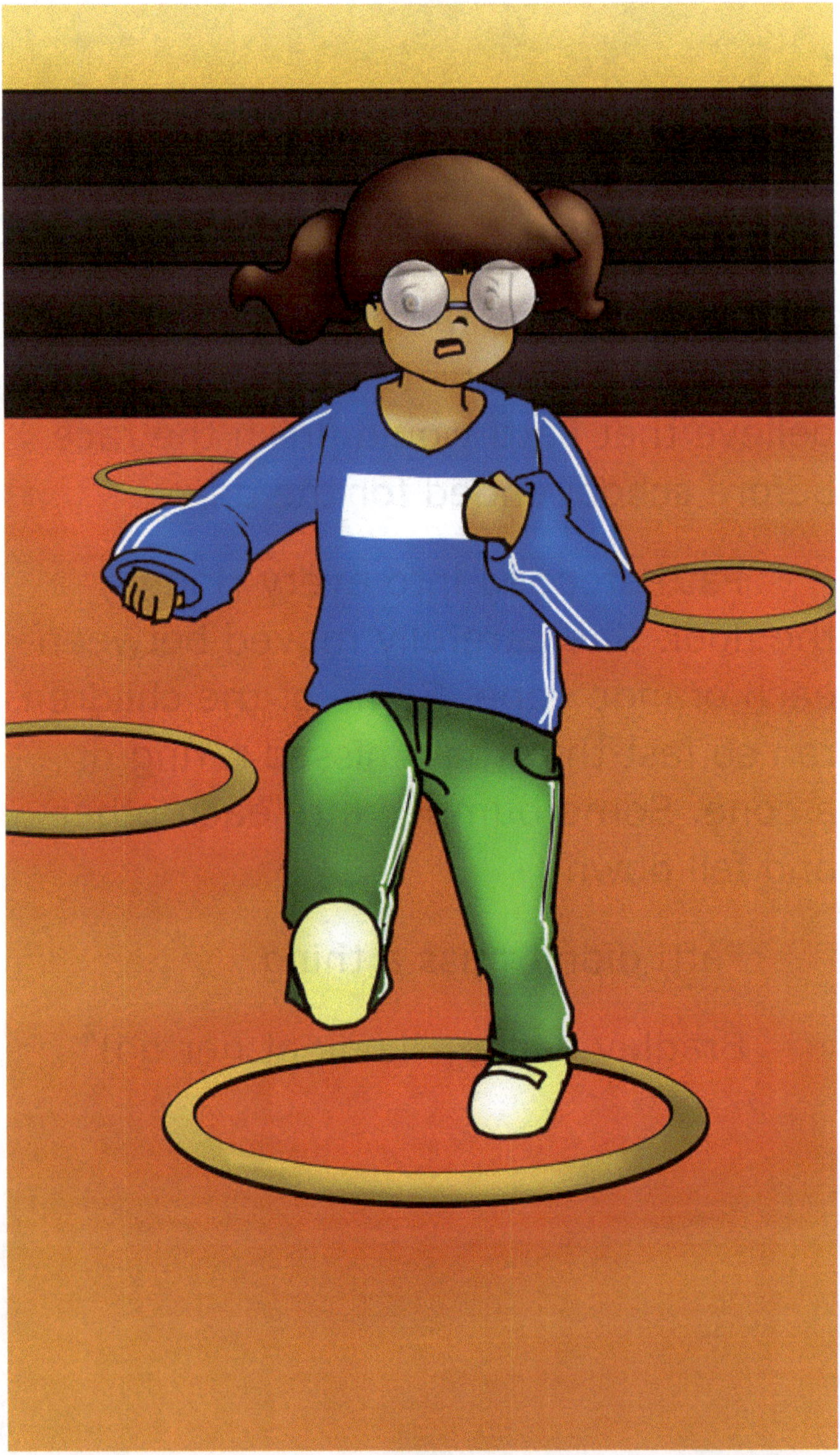

Their team won! The coach blew his whistle when Patti crossed the finish line. The four teammates took a victory lap around the gym. They waved to the fans in the stands.

Chapter 5
Friday

The schoolyard was covered with puddles. Children without boots tried not to get their feet wet. They weren't having much fun.

The boys circled Patti when she came down the stairs.

"Come with us. You're an Adventurer too," Bradley said. He stomped his black boot into a puddle. Water splashed everywhere.

"Adventurers. That's a good name." Allen grinned. Diego stomped his green boot in and Allen's blue boot joined them.

Patti jumped into the water with both yellow boots. They yelled, "Imagination activation!"

They hardly heard Mrs. Merkle saying, "Stop that splashing!"

They were far out in a tiny rowboat. Rain poured down. The ocean rolled and tossed their boat on wave after wave.

"Ship ahoy," Diego called, pointing.

A large ship floated not far away. The kids rowed hard. They got close to the ship and called for help. No one answered.

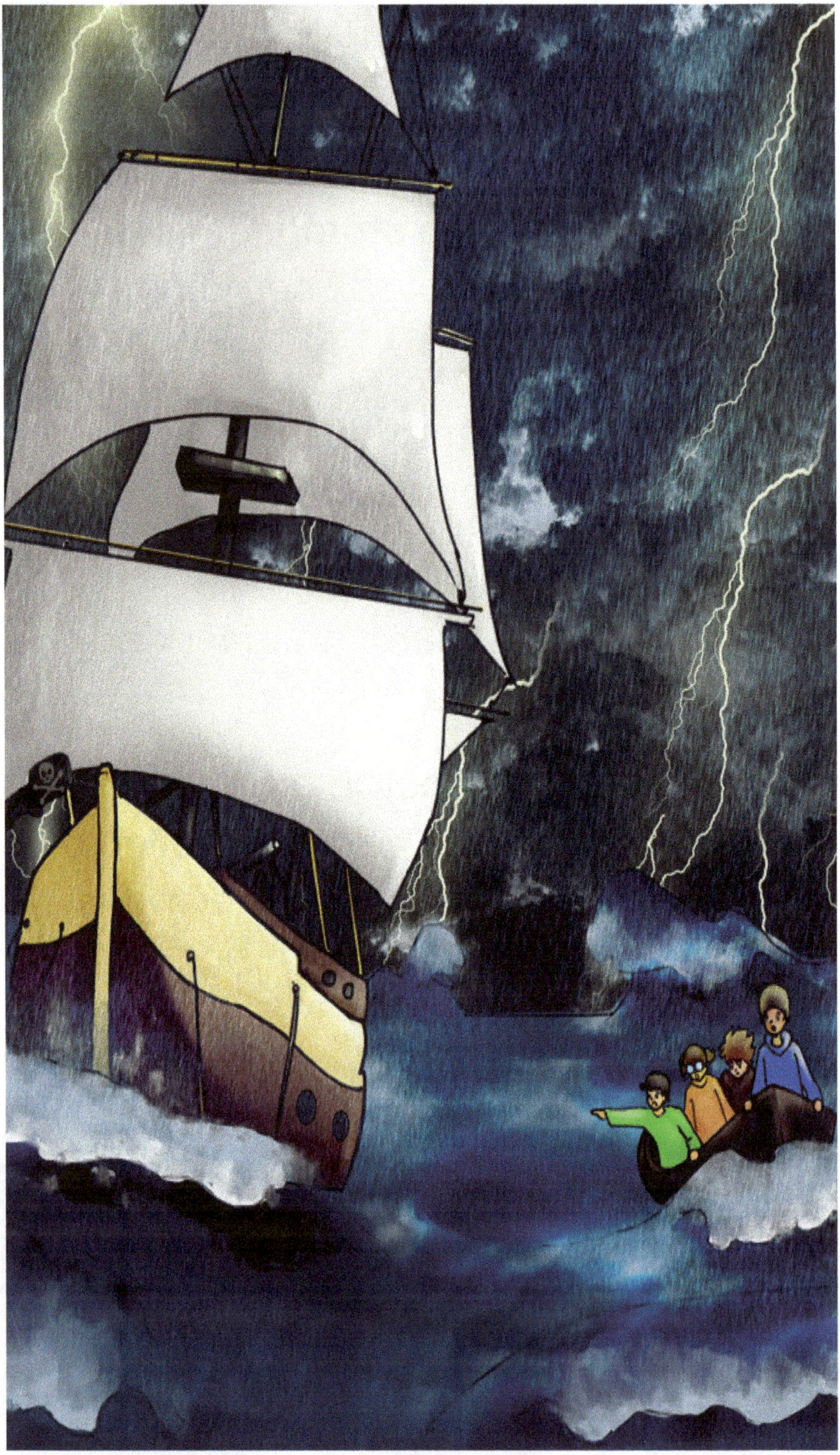

Patti said. "Let's get onboard. Maybe they're all inside."

They climbed a rope ladder to the deck. "There's no one here," Allen said. "We can go downstairs to get out of the rain." They found raincoats but no people.

They searched the ship from the bow to the stern. Then Bradley noticed the flag. The Jolly Roger!

"It's a pirate ship! This is NOT good," he said.

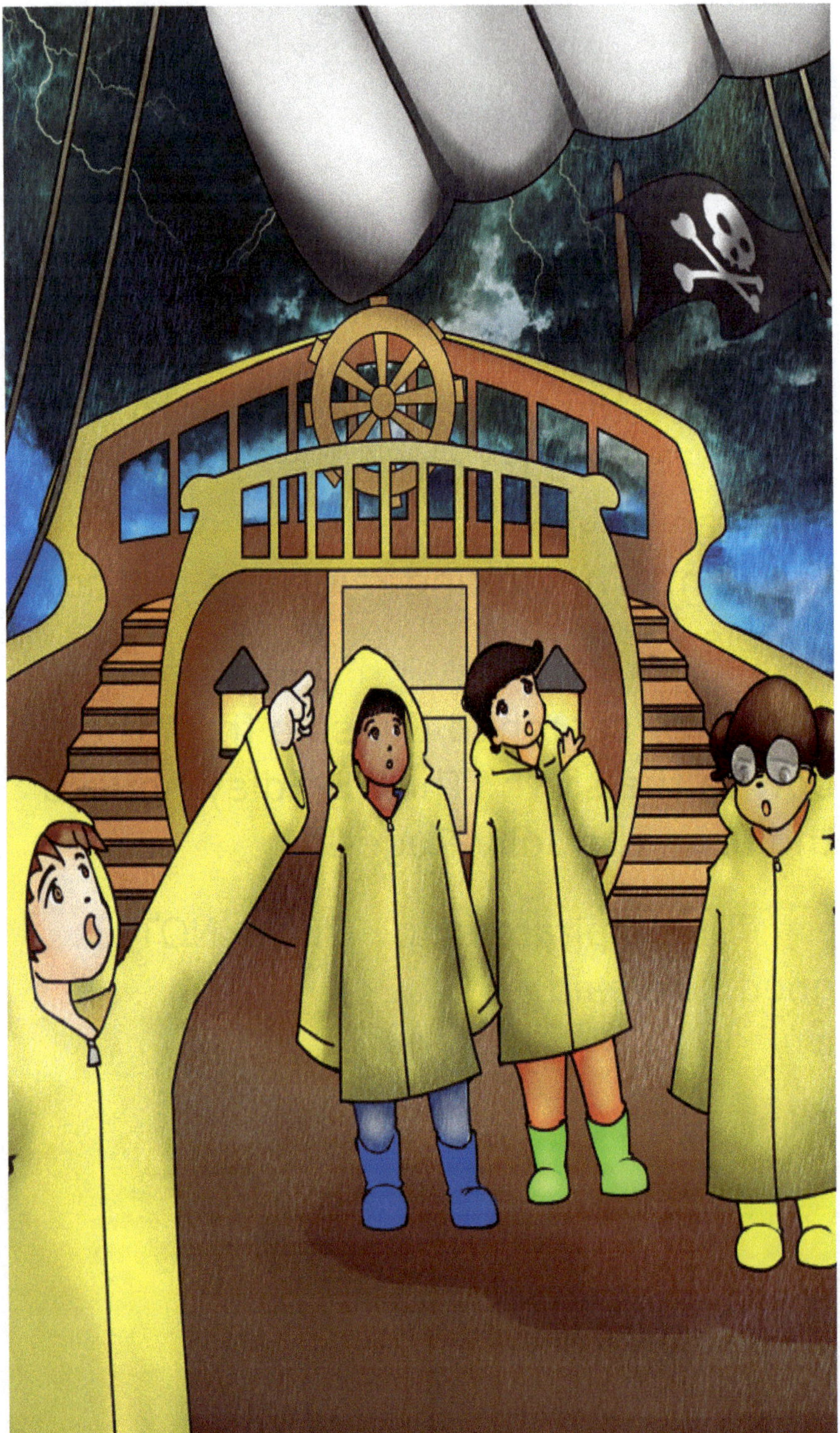

The wind swirled and howled. A man appeared. Then another and another.

"Pirates!" Diego shouted.

"Ghost pirates! Run!" Allen yelled.

The pirates chased them around the deck. The Adventurers ran up into the wheelhouse and down into the hold.

They were trapped!

"We need weapons. But how do you fight a ghost?" Bradley lifted the lid of a big wooden box.

"Sweet Puff Blunderbuss." Patti read the name.

"I've never seen a gun like that, even in the movies," Diego said.

Allen turned the gun over and looked at every side. "What does it shoot?"

"Those!" Patti reached into the box and then nibbled what she held. "Chocolate-covered marshmallows."

The boys crowded around to taste the candy too.

"Don't eat all the ammunition," Allen said.

BAM! BAM! There was a fierce knock on the hold door.

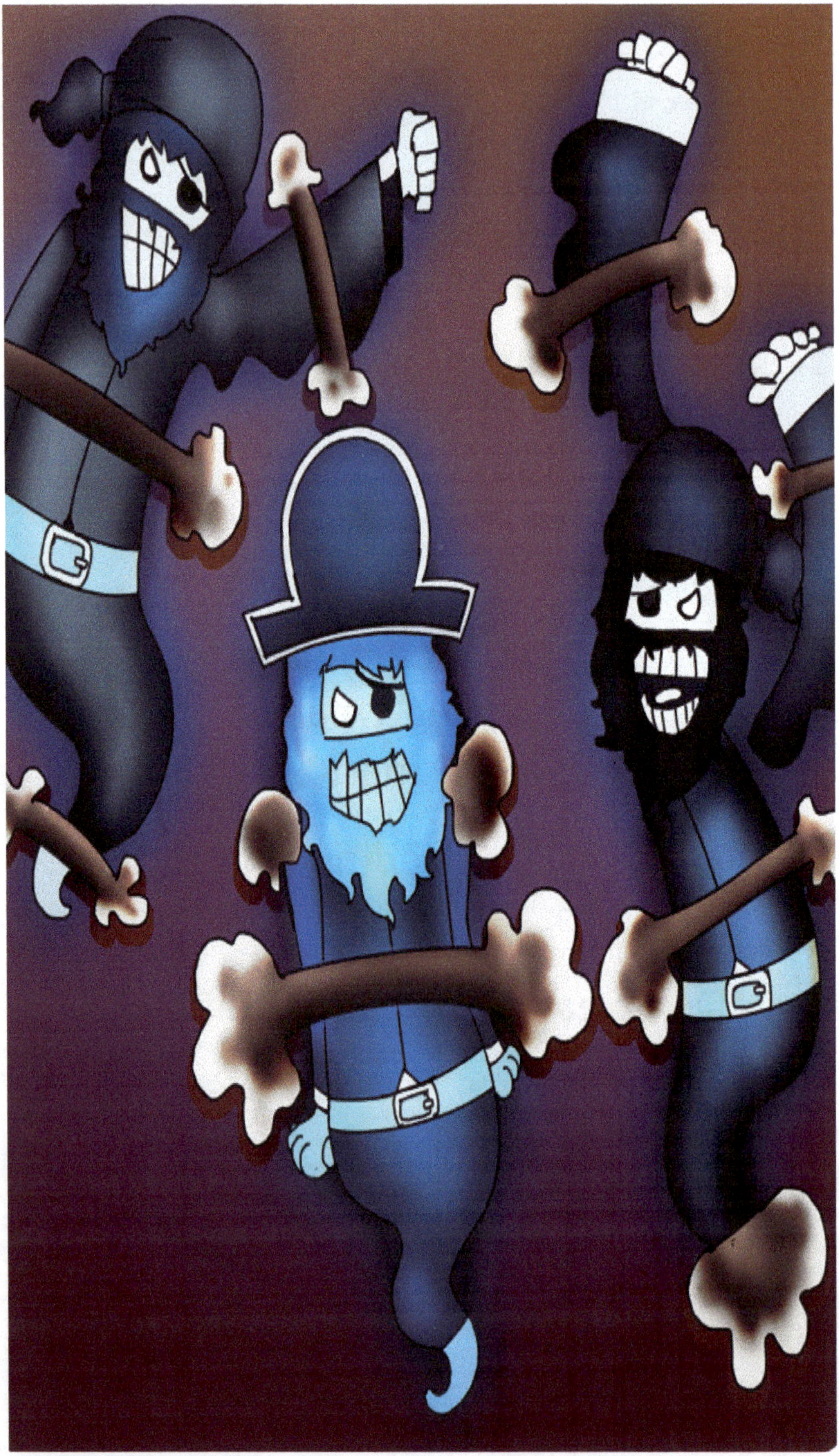

They tried to load the Blunderbusses fast. The sticky candy made it hard to do. The door came crashing down and the Adventurers fired.

The candy pinned the ghost pirates to the walls of the ship in ooey, gooey clumps. The Adventurers ran past them and jumped into the rowboat.

They got away just in time to hear, "Go wash your faces and hands. You know you're not supposed to have candy during school!"

The End

IMAGINATION ACTIVATION!™

Jenny Graham

Flying Turtle Publishing is delighted to partner with Jenny Graham for this book's activities. Her commitment to learning and her teaching experience make her especially qualified to create enhancement activities for *Adventures in Recess: The Boys*.

Jenny Graham is a qualified teacher with over 16 years of teaching experience. She has a love for reading and writing and this has instilled in her a passion towards creating the next generation of readers and writers. Jenny is the founder of abcJenny (http://jengraham71.wordpress.com/), a site which gives parents simple information and activities to help teach their children early reading and writing skills. She lives in a coastal town near Melbourne, Australia with her husband and two boys, Charlie and Tommy.

Follow us to fun activities!

Activity One – Comprehension

Educational Benefit: Reading Comprehension is an important skill of learning to read. To help children learn comprehension skills ask them direct questions about events which happened in the book, *Adventures in Recess*.

Activity: How well do you remember the book? Answer the following five questions. Circle the correct answer and find the word in the Word Search. Once you have found all five words, the left over letters reading left to right in the Word Search will spell a secret word.

On Monday Bradley, Diego and Allen were climbing along a fence, they looked down to see some hungry alligators. What were the alligators really?

   caterpillars   ants   stones

On Tuesday, why was it hard for them to walk on Magic Mountain?

   snow   water   grass

On Wednesday, the teacher sang, "One-two, buckle my ……………

   boot   belt   shoe

On Thursday, Patti, Allan, Bradley and Diego came what in the race?

   first   last   second

On Friday Diego, Allan, Bradley and Patti all stomped in the puddles with their what?

   shoes   boots   feet

WORD SEARCH

A	I	M	F	A	G
I	N	N	I	E	S
A	T	T	R	O	N
I	O	N	S	H	O
B	O	O	T	S	W

Activity Two – Word Skills

Educational Benefit: To encourage children to read longer words, one reading strategy is to find smaller words contained in the larger words.

Activity: The following words are in *Adventures in Recess*. Can you find all the smaller words in the bigger word? For example: the word "man" is in "Imagination." *You may easily find more than four words.*

Imagination 1. _____

2. _____

3. _____

4. _____

Adventures 1. _____

2. _____

3. _____

4. _____

Playground 1. _____

2. _____

3. _____

4. _____

Activation 1. _____

2. _____

3. _____

4. _____

Alligators   1. _____

                2. _____

                3. _____

                4. _____

Hopscotch   1. _____

                2. _____

                3. _____

                4. _____

Dragonfly   1. _____

                2. _____

                3. _____

                4. _____

Marshmallows 1. _____

                2. _____

                3. _____

                4. _____

Activity Three – Recess Super Hero

Educational Benefit: Thinking about others is an important social skill to teach children. Although it was part of the game, Diego thought about helping the younger student buckle her shoe.

Activity: Draw a picture of yourself as a Super Hero--remember to give yourself a name. Write the skills you have for helping others in the playground, such as helping younger students tie their shoelaces, picking up rubbish or finding a teacher if someone is hurt.

My Super Hero name is _____.

I help others by _____.

If you enjoyed Adventures in Recess, please leave a review on Goodreads, Amazon.com or leave us a comment at Flying Turtle Publishing.com. You can also find us on Facebook!

You might enjoy reading these books from Flying Turtle Publishing:

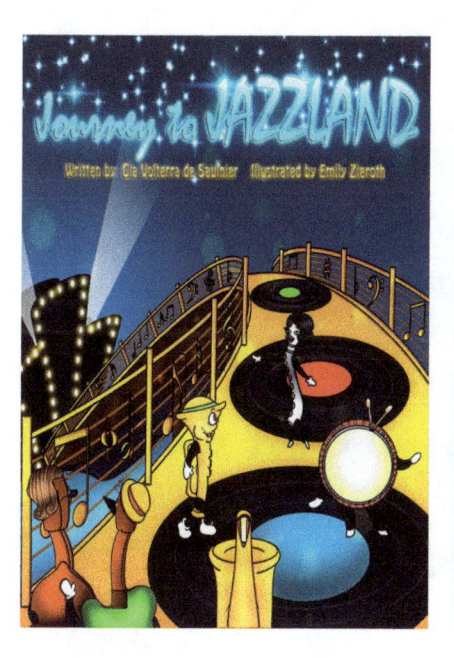

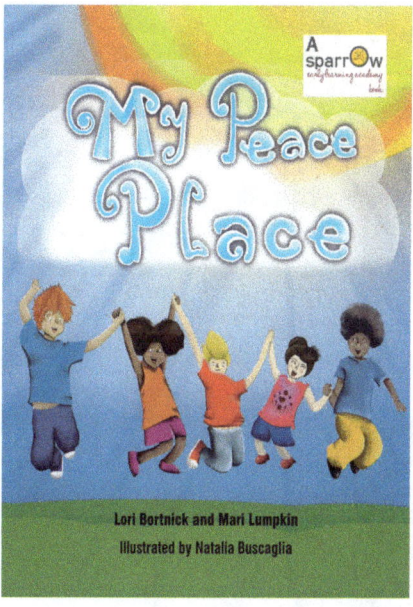

Printed in the USA
CPSIA information can be obtained
at www.ICGtesting.com
BVHW052340210823
668753BV00002B/15

9 780990 710431